William Alexander Hammond

**The Physics and Physiology of Spiritualism**

William Alexander Hammond

**The Physics and Physiology of Spiritualism**

ISBN/EAN: 9783337423452

Printed in Europe, USA, Canada, Australia, Japan

Cover: Foto ©Andreas Hilbeck / pixelio.de

More available books at **www.hansebooks.com**

THE

# PHYSICS AND PHYSIOLOGY

OF

# SPIRITUALISM.

BY

## WILLIAM A. HAMMOND, M. D.,

Professor of Diseases of the Mind and Nervous System, and of Clinical Medicine, in
the Bellevue Hospital Medical College; Physician-in-chief to the New York
State Hospital for Diseases of the Nervous System; Fellow of the College
of Physicians of Philadelphia; Member of the Academy of the Natural Sciences of Philadelphia; of the American Philosophical Society; of the Medical Society of the County of New York; of the
New York Medico-Legal Society; Honorary Member of
the British Medical Association; Corresponding Member of the Anthropological Society of London;
Member of the Verein Würtembergischer
Wundärzte und Geburtshelfer, etc., etc.

NEW YORK:

D. APPLETON & COMPANY,

90, 92 & 94 GRAND STREET.

1871.

THIS LITTLE VOLUME IS DEDICATED TO

MY FRIEND

JAMES R. WOOD, M. D., LL. D.,

EMERITUS PROFESSOR OF SURGERY IN THE BELLEVUE HOSPITAL MEDICAL
COLLEGE, NEW YORK,

WHOSE HONESTY OF PURPOSE

AND WHOSE SCIENTIFIC TRAINING WILL,

I AM SURE,

CAUSE HIM TO REGARD WITH FAVOR

AN ATTEMPT TO GIVE CORRECT IDEAS OF

A GREAT DELUSION.

# PREFACE.

THE basis of this monograph is an essay contributed to the *North American Review* for April, 1870.

Besides a very thorough revision, it has received large additions, which, it is hoped, will render it in some degree worthy of the good opinion with which it was originally honored.

162 West Thirty-fourth Street,
    NEW YORK, *October* 20, 1870.

# PHYSICS AND PHYSIOLOGY

## OF

# SPIRITUALISM.

---

## I.

THERE is an inherent tendency in the mind of man to ascribe to supernatural agencies those events the causes of which are beyond his knowledge ; and this is especially the case with the normal and morbid phenomena which are manifested in his own person. But, as his intellect becomes more thoroughly trained, and as science advances in its developments, the range of his credulity becomes more and more circumscribed, his doubts are multiplied, and he at length reaches that condition of "healthy skepticism" which allows of no belief without the proof. Thus he does not now credit the existence of an *archæus* dwelling in the stomach and presiding over its function, for he knows by experiment that digestion is a purely physical process, which can be as well performed in a teacup, with a little pepsin and dilute chlorhydric acid, as in the stomach with the gastric juice; he does not now believe that the bodies of lunatics, epileptics, and hysterical women, are inhabited by devils and demons, for he has ascertained by observation that the abnormal conditions present in such persons can be accounted for by material derangements of the organs or functions of the system.   He has learned to doubt, and, therefore, to reason better; he makes experiments, collects facts, does not begin to theorize until his data are sufficient, and then is careful that his theories do not extend beyond the foundation of certainty, or at least of probability, upon which he builds.

But there have always been, and probably always will be, individuals whose love for the marvellons is so great, and whose logical powers are so small, as to render them susceptible of entertaining any belief, no matter how preposterous it may be; and others, more numerous, who, staggered by facts which they cannot understand, accept any hypothesis which may be offered as an explanation, rather than confess their ignorance.

The real and fraudulent phenomena of what is called spiritualism are of such a character as to make a profound impression upon the credulous and the ignorant; and both these classes have accordingly been active in spreading the most exaggerated ideas relative to matters which are either absurdly false or not so very astonishing when viewed by the cold light of science. Such persons have, probably, from a very early age, believed in the materiality of spirits; and, having very little knowledge of the forces inherent in their own bodies, have no difficulty in ascribing occurrences,

which do not accord with their experience, to the agency of disembodied individuals whom they imagine to
be circulating through the world. In this respect they
resemble those savages who regard the burning-lens,
the mirror, and other things which produce unfamiliar
effects, as being animated by deities. Their minds
are decidedly fetish-worshipping in character, and are
scarcely, in this respect, of a more elevated type than
that of the Congo negro who endows the rocks and
trees with higher mental attributes than he claims for
himself.

Then it is possible for the most careful and experienced judgment to be deceived by false sensorial impressions of real objects, or by non-existing images created by
the mind. In the first case a gleam of moonlight passes
for a ghost, the stump of a tree becomes a robber, and
the rustling of leaves blown by the wind is imagined
to be the whispering of voices. No one possesses an
absolute perfection of sensation, and thus things are
never seen, or heard, or smelt, or tasted, or felt exactly
as they exist. In the dark, or in the uncertain light
of the moon, or of artificial illumination, the liability
to self-deception is very much increased ; and if, in ad-
dition to the defect of light, there are continual sounds
and other means of engaging the attention, it is exceedingly easy to induce sensorial confusion, and thus to
impose upon the intellect.

As regards purely imaginary images—that is, images not based on any sensorial impression—the difficulty is in the brain. An excess or deficiency of blood
circulating through this organ, or a morbid alteration

of its quality, such as is induced by alcohol, opium, belladonna, and other similar substances, will often lead to hallucinations. Those of De Quincey, Coleridge, and other opium-eaters, are well known, and several striking instances have come under my own notice.

Various mental emotions act in a like manner by their influence in deranging the central circulation. A young lady, who had overtasked her mind at school, was thrown thereby into a semi-hysterical condition, during which she saw spectres of various kinds which passed and repassed rapidly before her all day long. Every thing at which she looked appeared to her of enormous size. A head, for instance, seemed to be several feet in diameter, and little children looked like giants. When I took out my watch while examining her pulse, she remarked that it was as large as the wheel of a carriage. Sauvages refers to a somewhat similar case, in which a young woman, suffering from epilepsy, saw dreadful images, and to whom real objects appeared to be greatly magnified. A fly seemed as large as a chicken, and a chicken equalled an ox in size.

Physical causes, calculated to increase the amount of blood in the brain or to alter its quality, may give rise to hallucinations of various kinds. A gentleman, under the professional charge of the writer, can always cause the appearance of images by tying a handkerchief moderately tight around his neck; and there is one form which is always the first to come and the last to disappear. It consists of a male figure clothed in the costume worn in England three hundred years ago, and bearing a striking resemblance to the portraits of Sir

Walter Raleigh. This figure not only imposes on the sight, but also on the hearing; for questions put to it are answered promptly, and with much more intellectual force than those addressed to the so-called "spirits." How easy would it be for the gentleman subject to this hallucination, were he a believer in spiritualism, and less intelligent, to imagine that his visitor was a spirit, and that he held converse with the real Sir Walter Raleigh!

The fact that multitudes may be simultaneously impressed with the same belief, is no guaranty that this belief is founded on reality. A great many otherwise sensible people have been convinced that the blood of Saint Januarius periodically undergoes liquefaction; yet those, whose education and habits of thought teach them to look upon such so-called miracles with distrust, are not brought to accept the truth of the legend, because many thousands of other persons have received it in full faith.

There are two forces resulting from vitality, which may or may not be correlative, but which are of such a nature that some of their more unusual manifestations excite the astonishment of the vulgar, and are inexplicable to many who consider themselves learned. These are the mind and animal electricity. The latter, thanks to the investigations of Nobili, Matteucci, Müller, Du Bois-Reymond, and others, is beginning to be understood, and its phenomena reduced to fixed laws. All our knowledge of animal electricity tends to show that it does not differ in any essential particular from the galvanism developed outside of the body by chemical action; and that the tissues of the organism, the bones, muscles, nerves, etc., act toward it precisely as they do toward the galvanism which passes along an iron or copper wire and sets a telegraphic instrument in operation. It is impossible for us, therefore, to attribute any of the real or false manifestations of modern spiritualism to this force; and those persons who do so show themselves to be not fully acquainted either with what is asserted of spiritualism, or with electricity in its internal or external relations with the animal body. The idea that tables are moved, knocks made, and apparitions produced by the electricity of the body, is simply absurd.

The mind—under which term are included perception, the intellect, the emotions, and the will—is ordinarily supposed to have its seat wholly in the brain. That its higher manifestations are due to cerebral action is doubtless true; but holding the view that where there is gray nerve-tissue, there nervous power is generated, the writer believes—and physiology and pathology fully support the opinion—that the spinal cord and sympathetic system are capable of originating certain kinds of mental influence, which, when the brain is quiescent, may be wonderfully intensified. The physiology of the nervous system is by no means even tolerably well understood. Science has, for ages, been fettered by theological and metaphysical dogmas, which give the mind an existence independent of the nervous system, and which teach that it is an entity which sets all the functions of the body in action, and of which the brain is the seat. There can be no scientific inquiry relative to matters of faith—facts alone admit of investigation; and hence, so long as psychology was expounded by teachers who had never even seen a human brain, much less a spinal cord or sympathetic nerve, who knew absolutely nothing of nervous physiology, and who, therefore, taught from a standpoint which had not a single fact to rest upon, it was not to be expected that the true science of mind could make much progress. It is different now, but the great mass of physiologists have scarcely yet thrown off the trammels of the past, and, therefore, barely going a step in advance of Descartes—who confounded the mind with the soul, and lodged it in the pineal gland —they attribute all mental action to the brain alone.

Before we can be qualified to inquire into the powers of the mind, we must have a definite conception of what mind is. To express the idea in sufficiently full, but yet concise, language is difficult, and perhaps no definition can be given which will be entirely free from objection. For the purposes, however, of the present memoir, the mind may be regarded as a force the result of nervous action, and characterized by the ability to perceive sensations, to be conscious, to understand, to experience emotions, and to will in accordance therewith. Of these qualities consciousness resides exclusively in the brain, but the others, as is clearly shown by observation and experiment, cannot be restricted to this organ, but are developed with more or less intensity by other parts of the nervous system. It would be out of place to enter fully into the consideration of the important questions thus touched upon, but in the fact

that the spinal cord and sympathetic ganglia are not
devoid of mental power we find an explanation of some
of the most striking phenomena of what is called spiritualism.

## II.

It has been supposed that magnetism—a force correlative with electricity—resides in the body, and that
some persons are peculiarly sensitive to the influence of
the magnet and to the magnetism evolved by other individuals.  This subject has been thoroughly investigated by the Baron von Reichenbach, a very learned, but
certainly a very imaginative man, who has developed
from his inquiries some truth and a great deal of fancy.
He sought to give an explanation of mesmerism, and
really succeeded, to a certain extent.  The following
observation is certainly true :

" If a strong magnet, capable of supporting about
ten pounds, be drawn downward over the bodies of
fifteen or twenty persons, without actually touching
them, some among them will always be found to be
excited by it in a peculiar manner.  The number of
people who are sensitive in this way is greater than is
generally imagined. . . . The kind of impression produced on these excitable people, who otherwise may be
regarded as in perfect health, is scarcely describable ; it
is rather disagreeable than pleasant, and combined with
a slight sensation of cold or warmth, resembling a cool
or gently warm breath of air, which the patients imagine to blow softly upon them.  Sometimes they feel
sensations of drawing, pricking, or creeping ; some

complain of sudden attacks of headache. Not only women, but men in the very prime of life, are found distinctly susceptible to this influence; in children it is sometimes very active." *

Reichenbach supposed that these and other phenomena were due to a hitherto undescribed force which he denominated *od*, the *odic force*, or *odyle*, and which was present in the body. When evolved in large quantity, the subjects were said to be sensitive, and could then not only experience the sensations mentioned, but could also see the luminous flames which were asserted to be given off from the poles of a magnet. At first his experiments were conducted with confessedly sickly persons; but he subsequently ascertained that individuals in perfect health were capable of experiencing the same sensations. What the baron's "perfect health" was will be apparent from the following remarks, which conclude his detailed description of thirty-five persons who were thus doubly gifted:

"None of these perfectly healthy persons knew any thing about their most remarkable and interesting peculiarities; and they were not a little astonished at the discovery, under my guidance, of powers of which they had never before dreamed. The manner in which I come upon the trace of them, which I at once take up and follow, is now simply this: I inquire among my acquaintance whether they know any one who is frequently troubled with periodical headaches, especially

---

* Physico-Physiological Researches on the Dynamics of Magnetism, etc., p. 3. English translation, by Dr. John Ashburner. London, 1851.

megrim, who complains of temporary oppression of the stomach, or who often sleeps badly without apparent cause, talks in the sleep, rises up or even gets out of bed, or is restless at night during the period of full moon, or to whom the moonlight in general is disagreeable, or who is readily disordered in churches or theatres, or very sensitive to strong smells, grating or shrill noises, etc.,—all such persons, who may be otherwise healthy, I seek after, and make a pass with a finger over the palm of their hands, and scarcely ever miss finding them sensitive. When they follow me into the obscurity of my dark chamber and remain there an hour or two, their surprise is excited by the appearance of a quantity of luminous appearances, of which they had not previously the slightest idea. The number of persons who are in this state of excitability does actually exceed belief, and I state it rather below than above the reality when I say that at least a third part of the population are sensitive; for on every side on which I turn I meet with healthy sensitives; and I could in a few days collect, not dozens, but hundreds, if it were requisite. It will and must soon be proved how little ground there is to doubt these asseverations. Sensitiveness is not a rarity among human beings, as I myself thought some years ago, but a very generally distributed quality, which, after my accounts, will soon be discovered in every direction, and will throw open a new and not unimportant page of the human condition."

Can any physician conversant with the abnormal conditions of the nervous system doubt that such

" healthy persons " as those described by the Baron von Reichenbach could be made, "under guidance," to see or feel almost any thing suggested to them? The writer has now under his professional care a young lady, hysterical, a somnambulist, and affected with chorea, upon whom this principle of suggestion can be made to act with striking effect, and who would be a perfect godsend to all mesmerizers, mediums, and electro-biologists. For instance, it is only necessary to tell her that certain images are before her, when she directly sees them exactly as they are described; to inform her that she is about to have galvanism applied, and then to give her the unconnected poles, when she at once experiences the shock; to ask her if she has not a bitter or a sweet or a sour taste in her mouth, when she immediately declares that she has just such a taste as is mentioned. Voices are heard and odors smelt precisely as they are described to her. Hundreds of patients affected with diseases of the nervous system are susceptible, in a greater or less degree, to the operation of suggestion; and to the action of this principle many miracles and impostures owe the success with which they have been received. To it many of the phenomena of spiritualism are clearly due.

But notwithstanding the fact that many of the experiments of the Baron von Reichenbach have no other foundation than that property of the human mind which causes it to be subjectively affected by suggestion, it is undoubtedly true that there is a germ of fact in his investigations, and that magnetism is destined to play an important part in physiology and pathology. In a strikingly original and interesting paper * recently published, the experiments detailed in which have been verified by the writer, it is clearly shown that certain very obvious symptoms are induced by the application of a magnet to the body, and that the lower animals and even plants are indubitably affected by its influence.

But with all this there is no proof that magnetism or the odic force is capable under any circumstances of producing the clairvoyant state, of moving tables, of causing raps, or that any of the other more striking phenomena that are claimed for spiritualism can be accounted for through its agency. The *possibility* of such a power being exercised is quite another thing. The force that can cause a mass of iron to be moved in opposition to the laws of gravity, and through media impervious to all ordinary influences, can scarcely have the word *impossible* applied to it. But this is not a question of possibilities, but of facts, and certainly it has not been shown, with that reasonable degree of certainty which all scientific questions demand, that magnetism in or out of the body exercises any such control over mind or matter as has been claimed by its partisans.

The attention, when concentrated upon any particular thing or part of the body, will often lead to erroneous sensorial impressions. An observer gazing anxiously out to sea, or across a vast plain, will scarcely ever fail to see the object of which he is in search ; an

* " On the Physiological Action of Magnetism." By John Vansant, M. D., etc., Journal of Psychological Medicine, April, 1870.

expectant watcher hears every moment the rumbling of wheels, the footstep, or the knock which announces the wished-for or dreaded arrival; and pains, tastes, odors, and even diseases, can frequently be thus originated. Thus, a lady who has been under the professional care of the writer for intense nervous headaches, and who is of a very impressionable organization, is able at will to produce a pain in any part of her body by steadily fixing her attention upon it. Even the mention in her presence of physical suffering experienced by other persons immediately results in her feeling similar pains to those described, in corresponding parts of her own body. The case of Mrs. A., detailed by Sir David Brewster,* is a forcible illustration of the point in question.

Physicians know very well that actual organic disease may be produced by the habitual concentration of the attention on an organ. The fancies of the hypochondriac may thus in time become realities.

Many of the facts of spiritualism are clearly explainable by referring them to this influence.

### III.

A still more important factor in the production of spiritualistic manifestations is sleight-of-hand. The perfection to which this art is carried by accomplished performers is really remarkable, and is much more wonderful than would be real visitations of spirits. The knowledge of human nature and of practical science

---

* Letters on Natural Magic addressed to Sir Walter Scott, Letter III.

requisite for some feats of legerdemain is necessarily very great, and the manipulations often require a degree of dexterity which cannot fail to excite astonishment. It is a well-known fact that the art in question can be satisfactorily made to explain many operations apparently supernatural, and that "mediums" do not hesitate to avail themselves of its resources. They are most of them, however, sorry performers, when compared with East-Indian jugglers, and with some who make no secret of the fact that their performances are deceptions.

A short time since, I invited several medical and other friends to witness, in my library, some surprising spiritualistic exhibitions by a first-class "medium." The operator went through all the performances of the Davenport brothers, to the entire satisfaction of the audience. He was securely tied by a gentleman who had been an officer in the naval service, and who exhausted his strength and ingenuity in devising bands and knots; a screen was then placed in front of the "medium," and, in an instant, an accordeon was played, a bell rung, and a tambourine struck. The performer then requested that the screen might be removed, and, on this being done, he was found to be tied in precisely the same manner as at first. The gentleman who had bound him declared that not a cord or a knot had been interfered with. In a second attempt the "medium," tied with additional care, rang a bell and was discovered intact in a second afterward.

The "rapping" of this gentleman was perfect, and he read communications from the dead, made on folded

slips of paper, with a skill equal to that of the most orthodox and highly-gifted medium.

The astonishment of the audience was great when
he informed them that all his performances were deceptions, which he then proceeded to explain in the most
satisfactory manner.

Those who desire an evening's amusement cannot
procure it more satisfactorily than by requesting Dr.
Von Vleck to enlighten them in regard to spiritualism.

## IV.

There is a condition known as somnambulism, into
which persons of impressionable nervous systems are
prone to pass, and which in such individuals may
readily be induced by artificial means. In this state
certain faculties and senses are intensely exalted, and
if the attention can be concentrated upon any particular idea, circumstance, or object, great lucidity is manifested. On the other hand, there may be, and generally
is, the most profound abstraction of mind in regard to
all other ideas or things.

The most thorough work on natural somnambulism
is that of Bertrand,* published nearly fifty years ago,
but which is still admirable for the truthful account of
the various phenomena attendant upon the condition
in question. Bertrand assigns somnambulism to four
causes:

---

* "Traité du Somnambulisme et des différentes Modifications quil'
présente." Paris, 1823.

1. A particular nervous temperament, which pre-disposes individuals otherwise in good health to parox-ysms of somnambulism during their ordinary sleep.

2. It is sometimes produced in the course of certain diseases, of which it may be considered a symptom or a crisis.

3. It is often seen in the course of the proceeding necessary to bring on the condition known as animal magnetism.

4. It may result as a consequence of a high degree of mental exaltation. It is in this state contagious by imitation to such persons as are submitted to the same influence.

From these four categories of causes Bertrand distinguishes four kinds of somnambulism—the natural, the symptomatic, the artificial, and the ecstatic. Under the artificial variety we must include Mr. Braid's hyp-notism. In general terms, therefore, there are two kinds of somnambulism, the natural and the artificial. As an instance of the former condition, the follow-ing case is adduced from a recent monograph of the writer : *

" A young lady of great personal attractions had the misfortune to lose her mother by death from chol-era. Several other members of the family suffered from the disease, she alone escaping, though almost worn out with fatigue, excitement, and grief. A year after these events her father removed from the West to New York, bringing her with him and putting her at the head of his household. She had not been

* "Sleep and its Derangements," p. 205. Philadelphia, 1869.

long in New York before she became affected with symptoms resembling those met with in chorea. The muscles of the face were in almost constant action; and though she had not altogether lost the power to control them by her will, it was difficult at times for her to do so. She soon began to talk in her sleep, and finally was found one night by her father, as he came home, endeavoring to open the street door. She was then, as he said, sound asleep, and had to be violently shaken to be aroused. After this she made the attempt every night to get out of bed, but was generally prevented by a nurse who slept in the same room with her, and who was awakened by the noise she made. Her father now consulted me in regard to the case, and invited me to the house in order to witness the somnambulic acts for myself. One night, therefore, I went to his residence, and waited for the expected manifestations. The nurse had received orders not to interfere with her charge on this occasion, unless it was evident that injury would result, and to notify us of the beginning of the performance.

"About twelve o'clock she came down-stairs and informed us that the young lady had risen from her bed and was about to dress herself. I went up-stairs, accompanied by her father, and met her in the upper hall partly dressed. She was walking very slowly and deliberately, her head elevated, her eyes open, and her hands hanging loosely by her side. We stood aside to let her pass. Without noticing us, she descended the stairs to the parlor, we following her. Taking a match which she had brought with her from her own room

she rubbed it several times on the under side of the
mantel-piece until it caught fire, and then, turning on
the gas, lit it. She next threw herself into an arm-
chair and looked fixedly at a portrait of her mother
which hung over the mantel-piece. While she was in
this position I carefully examined her countenance,
and performed several experiments, with the view of
ascertaining the condition of the senses as to activity.

"She was very pale, more so than was natural to
her; her eyes were wide open, and did not wink when
the hand was brought suddenly in close proximity to
them; the muscles of the face, which, when she was
awake, were almost constantly in action, were now perfectly still; her pulse was regular in rhythm and force,
and beat eighty-two per minute, and the respiration
was uniform and slow.

"I held a large book between her eyes and the pic-
ture she was apparently looking at, so that she could
not see it. She nevertheless continued to gaze in the
same direction as if no obstacle were interposed. I
then made several motions as if about to strike her in the
face. She made no attempt to ward off the blows, nor
did she give the slightest sign that she saw my actions.
I touched the corner of each eye with a lead-pencil I
had in my hand, but even this did not make her close
her eyelids. I was entirely satisfied that she did not
see, at least with her eyes.

"I held a lighted sulphur-match under her nose, so
that she could not avoid inhaling the sulphurous acid
gas which escaped. She gave no evidence of feeling
any irritation. Cologne and other perfumes and smell-

ing-salts likewise failed to make any obvious impression on her olfactory nerves.

"Through her partially-opened mouth I introduced a piece of bread soaked in lemon-juice. She evidently failed to perceive the sour taste. Another piece of bread saturated with a solution of quinine was equally ineffectual. The two pieces remained in her mouth a full minute and were then chewed and swallowed.

"She now arose from her chair and began to pace the room in an agitated manner; she wrung her hands, sobbed, and wept violently. While she was acting in this way, I struck two books together several times so as to make loud noises close to her ears. This failed to interrupt her.

"I then took her by the hand and led her back to the chair in which she had previously been sitting. She made no resistance, but sat down quietly and soon became perfectly calm.

"Scratching the back of her hand with a pin, pulling her hair, and pinching her face, appeared to excite no sensation.

"I then took off her slippers and tickled the soles of her feet. She at once drew them away, but no laughter was produced. As often as this experiment was repeated, the feet were drawn up. The spinal cord was therefore awake.

"She had now been down-stairs about twenty minutes. Desiring to awake her, I shook her by the shoulders quite violently for several seconds without success.

I then took her head between my hands and shook it. This proved effectual in a little while. She awoke

2

suddenly, looked around her for an instant, as if endeavoring to comprehend her situation, and then burst
into a fit of hysterical sobbing. When she recovered
her equanimity she had no recollection of any thing
that had passed, or of having had a dream of any
kind."

This case illustrates very well some of the principal
phenomena of natural somnambulism. Many others
are on record which, in many respects, are more remarkable, but it is scarcely necessary to refer to them
here at greater length.

Now, it has long been known that somnambulism
can be artificially induced. Even before the time of
Mesmer there were occasional illustrations of this fact;
but Puysegur is entitled to the credit of being the first
to systematize them and to practise the art of producing factitious somnambulism. He caused it by passes,
and finally, it is claimed, by simple acts of the will.
The Abbé Faria induced it by shouting, and Barberin
by praying! Other methods were also employed; and,
as its identity with mesmerism became generally recognized, it had ascribed to it the name of mesmeric or
magnetic sleep.

No one has more thoroughly investigated the nature
of artificial somnambulism than Mr. Braid,* who gives
the following as his ordinary method of procedure:

" Take any bright object (I generally use my lancet-
case) between the thumb and fore and middle fingers
of the left hand, hold it from eight to fifteen inches

---

* "Neurypnology, or the Rationale of Nervous Sleep, considered in
Relation with Animal Magnetism," etc.  London, 1843.

from the eyes at such position above the forehead as may be necessary to produce the greatest possible strain upon the eyes and eyelids, and enable the patient to maintain a steady, fixed stare at the object. It will generally be found that the eyelids close with a *vibratory* motion, or become spasmodically closed. After ten or fifteen seconds have elapsed, by gently elevating the arms and legs, it will be found that the patient has a disposition to retain them in the situation in which they have been placed, if he is intensely affected. If this is not the case, desire him to retain the limbs in the extended position, and thus the pulse will speedily become greatly accelerated, and the limbs, in process of time, become quite rigid and involuntarily fixed. It will also be found that all the organs of special sense, excepting sight, including heat, and cold, and muscular motion or resistance, are *at first* prodigiously *exalted*, such as happens with regard to the primary effects of opium, wine, and spirits. After a certain point, however, this exaltation of function is followed by a state of depression far greater than the torpor of *natural* sleep. From the state of the most profound torpor of the organs of special sense and tonic rigidity of the muscles, they may at this stage *instantly* be restored to the *opposite* condition of extreme mobility and exalted sensibility, by directing a current of air against the organ or organs we wish to excite to action or the muscles we wish to render limber, and which had been in this cataleptiform state. By mere repose the senses will speedily merge into the original condition again."

Mr. Braid gives examples of this artificial somnambulism or hypnotism, as he designates it, which show that its phenomena are identical with those of natural somnambulism, and that it covers much that is alleged to be due to animal magnetism and modern spiritualism. He found the same condition to be produced, though he left the room, if the subject followed his directions, so that there could be no suspicion that he acted through the medium of any force emanating from his body.

The persons who most readily come into the hypnotic condition are of the same class as those who were such favorable subjects for the odic force of Von Reichenbach, and who now make the best mediums. The writer has very carefully investigated this division of the subject, and has made many experiments in regard to it, which leave no doubt in his mind that the relation really exists. As an illustration of the character of the phenomena, the following case is adduced. He does not doubt that the thoughtful reader will at once see, that if such a person, as the one whose actions while in the hypnotic state are described, should be disposed to deceive, or should be under the control of designing or ignorant individuals, she would not fail to be received by many as a medium of the first order.

A short time after writing the account of the young lady whose case has just been quoted as an example of natural somnambulism, I was informed by her father that her affection, which had been cured by suitable medical treatment, had returned, owing, as he supposed, to excessive mental exertion, she having contracted a taste for philosophy, in the study of which she had indulged to a great extent.

Upon examination, I found that she not only had paroxysms of natural somnambulism, but that she had acquired the power of inducing the hypnotic state at will. Her process was to take up some one of the philosophical works she was in the habit of studying, select a paragraph which required intense thought or excited powerful emotion, read it, close the book, fix her eyes steadily, but not directing the foci so as to see any particular object, and then reflect deeply upon what she had read. From the revery thus occasioned, she gradually passed into the somnambulic condition. During this state it was said she answered questions correctly, read books held behind her, described scenes passing in distant places, and communicated messages from the dead. She therefore possessed, in every essential respect, the qualifications of either a clairvoyant or a spiritualistic medium, according to the peculiar tenets of belief held by the faithful.

In accordance with my request, she proceeded to put herself into the hypnotic state. With a volume of Plato in her hand, she read thus from the Apology of Socrates. Her voice was calm and impressive, as though she felt every word she uttered :

"Moreover, we may hence conclude that there is great hope that death is a blessing. For to die is one of two things : for either the dead may be annihilated and have no sensation of any thing whatever, or, as it is said, there is a certain change and passage of the soul from one place to another. And if it is a privation of

all sensation, as it were a sleep in which the sleeper has
no dream, death would be a wonderful gain. For I
think that if any one having selected a night in which
he slept so soundly as not to have had a dream, and
having compared this night with all the other nights
and days of his life, should be required on consideration
to say how many days and nights he had passed better
and more pleasantly than this night throughout his life,
I think that not only a private person, but even the
great king himself, would find them easy to number in
comparison with other days and nights. If, therefore,
death is a thing of this kind, I say it is a gain; for thus
all futurity appears to be nothing more than one night."

As she reached the close, her voice became inex-
pressibly sad, the book dropped from her hand, her
eyes were fixed on vacancy, her hands lay quietly in
her lap, her breath came irregularly, and tears were
flowing down her cheeks. Her pulse, which before she
began to read was eighty-four per minute, was now
one hundred and eight. As her abstraction became
more profound, it fell, till, when she was unconscious,
three minutes after she ceased reading, it was only sev-
enty-two.

To satisfy myself that she was completely hyp-
notized, I held a bottle of strong *aqua ammoniæ* to
her nostrils. She did not evince the slightest degree
of sensibility. Touching the eye with the finger—a
test that a person practising deception could not have
borne—equally failed to afford the least response indic-
ative of sensation. I was, therefore, satisfied that she
was in the condition of artificial somnambulism.

To describe in detail all that took place would lengthen unduly this paper; such parts, therefore, as are material, and which illustrate essential points, will alone be given.

The writer asked her if there were any spirits in the room.

" Yes."

" Whose spirits are they ? "

" The spirit of Socrates is here, the spirit of Plato, the spirit of Schleiermacher." (She had been reading before my arrival " Schleiermacher's Introductions to the Dialogues of Plato.")

" Do you not also see the spirit of Schenkelfürst ? "

This was a *ruse*, there being no such person.

" Schenkelfürst ? " she asked.

" Yes ; he was Schleiermacher's constant companion and friend."

" Schenkelfürst," she repeated ; " what a singular name ! "

She was silent for a moment, and then her face was lit up with a smile, and she exclaimed :

" I see him ; he is a small, dark man, with sharp, piercing eyes ; he wears a coat trimmed with fur ; he approaches Schleiermacher ; they embrace ; they are talking to each other."

" Will not Schleiermacher send some message through you ? "

" No ; he has gone away with his friend."

" Will no other spirit communicate ? "

" Yes, there is one coming now ; a man with a mournful face ; his name is Bruno—Giordano Bruno.

He speaks; he says, 'O my friends, be of good cheer; there is no end, even as there has been no beginning; the weak-hearted fall from the ranks, and, for a time, are lost; but, as there is a portion of the divinity in all God's creatures, even they are regenerated.' "

She stopped, and then in a low voice said, while tears streamed down her cheeks:

"*Majori forsitan cum timore sententiam in me fertis quam ego accipiam*"—the words used by Bruno when sentence of death was pronounced upon him. She had finished reading his life a few weeks before.

Desiring to change the current of her thoughts, and also to test her powers of prevision, she was asked who would be the first patient to enter the office of the writer that day week, and with what disease would he or she be affected?

She answered promptly:

"A gentleman from Albany, I see him now; he is thin and pale, and very weak; he is lame, I think he is paralyzed."

The first person in reality who entered the office on the day in question was a lady of New York, suffering from nervous headache.

She was then asked where her father was at that moment (4.10 P. M.). Her answer was: "At the corner of Wall Street and Broadway; he is looking at the clock on Trinity Church; he is waiting for a stage." During the hour between four o'clock and five her father was in Brooklyn.

A table with paper was now placed before her, a pencil put into her hand, and she was requested again to place herself *en rapport* with some spirit. She immediately began to write as follows: "Let all the world hear my voice and follow the precepts I inculcate. There are many fools and but few wise. I write for the former, and am probably a fool myself, for I constantly see a chasm yawning at my side; and though my intellect tells me there is no chasm near me, I place a screen so that I cannot see it. PASCAL." She had that very day been reading a memoir of Pascal, in which the hallucination referred to was mentioned.

The following conversation then took place:

"Where are you now?"

"In New York."

"No, you are in a vessel at sea; there is a terrible storm; are you not afraid?"

"Yes, I am very much frightened; what shall I do? Oh, save me, save me!"

She wrung her hands, screamed with terror, rose from her chair and paced the room, apparently suffering intensely from fear. In the midst of her agitation she awoke, and it was not without difficulty that the impression she had received could be removed.

On a subsequent occasion her somnambulic powers of vision were tested by asking her to read the writing on a slip of paper; to tell the time marked by a watch held to the back of her head; to read a particular line from a closed book, etc.; but, though she always made some answer, she was never once right. The senses of touch and of hearing were the only ones she appeared to be capable of exercising, and these were not in any degree exalted in their action. Conjoined with integ-

rity of touch there was well-marked *analgesia*, or inability to feel pain. Thus, though able to tell the shape,
texture, and consistence of objects placed in her hands,
she experienced no sensation when a pin was thrust into
the calf of her leg, or when a coal of fire was held in
close proximity to any part of her body.

It will readily be preceived, therefore, that certain
parts of her nervous system were in a state of inaction,
were in fact dormant, while others remained capable of
receiving sensations and originating nervous influence.
Her sleep was therefore incomplete. Images were
formed, hallucinations entertained, and she was accordingly in these respects in a condition similar to that of
a dreaming person; for the images and hallucinations
were either directly connected with thoughts she had
previously had, or were immediately suggested to her
through her sense of hearing. Some mental faculties
were exercised, while others were quiescent. There
was no correct judgment and no volition. Imagination, memory, the emotions, and *the ability to be impressed by suggestions*, were present in a high degree.

Now, the writer is satisfied, from a careful study of
this lady's case, and of others similar to it in general
character which have come under his observation, that
the phenomena of hypnotism are not those of pure somnambulism, but that three other conditions are present
in greater or less degree. These are hysteria, catalepsy,
and ecstasy. To a brief consideration of some of the
more important features of these abnormal states of the
nervous system the attention of the reader is invited,

with the expectation that they will be found to account for many of the phenomena of spiritualism.

## V.

There is a strong tendency, in all persons affected with hysteria, to the occurrence of symptoms which simulate organic diseases. Paralysis, both of motion and of sensation, is one of the morbid conditions thus assumed. This tendency is not generally voluntary, though undoubtedly cases are not infrequent in which the simulation is clearly intentional, and others more numerous in which volition, when brought to bear with full force upon the disposition, will overcome it. In these latter cases there is, as it were, a paralysis of the will. In other instances hysterical persons will deliberately enter upon a systematic course of deception and fraud, more, apparently, for the sake of attracting attention and obtaining notoriety than from any other motive.

Thus an hysterical woman will suddenly take to her bed and declare that she has no feeling and no power of motion in her leg or arm. The most careful examination shows that she is speaking the truth. Pins may be thrust into the affected limb, it may be pinched or scorched *ad libitum*, and yet the possessor does not wince. A somewhat analogous state exists in us at all times. When the mind is intensely occupied or the passions greatly aroused, there is the same insensibility to pain. Many a soldier has not discovered his wound till the heat of the battle was over.

Now, when great mental exaltation is induced in an hysterical person we find this analgesic condition developed to its utmost extent. Under these combined influences weak girls have submitted to all kinds of maltreatment and suffered no pain, and have been able to resist blows and other bodily injuries which in their normal condition would have caused death. Thus it is stated by Montgeron,* in his account of the Jansenist Convulsionnaires, that some women gave themselves severe blows with iron instruments in such a manner that sharp points were forced into the flesh. Fouillou states that another had herself hung up by the heels with the head downward, and remained in this position three-quarters of an hour. One day as she lay extended on her bed two men who held a cloth under her back raised her up and threw her forward two thousand four hundred times, while two other persons placed in front thrust her back. Another day four men having taken hold of her by the extremities began to pull her, each with all his strength, and she was thus dragged in different directions for the space of some minutes. She caused herself to be tied one day as she lay on the table, her arms crossed behind her back and her legs flexed to their fullest extent, and, while six men struck her without ceasing, a seventh choked her. After this she remained insensible for some time, and her tongue, inflamed and discolored, hung far out of her mouth. Another insisted upon receiving a hundred blows upon the stomach with an andiron, and these were so heavy that

* La Vérité des Miracles, tome ii. 1737. Quoted by Calmeil, De la Folie, etc. Paris, 1845.

they shook the wall against which she was placed, and upon one occasion a breach in it was caused at the twenty-fifth blow.

A physician, hearing of these things, insisted that they could not be true, as it was physically impossible that the skin, the flesh, the bones, and the internal organs, could resist such violence. He was told to come and verify the facts. He hastened to do so, and was struck with astonishment. Scarcely believing his eyes, he begged to be allowed to administer the blows. A strong iron instrument, sharp at one end, was put into his hands; he struck with all his might and thrust it deep into the flesh, but the victim laughed at his efforts, and remarked that his blows only did her good.

This immunity from injury, though remarkable, is frequently met with among hysterical persons at the present day, but is much more frequently assumed. Calmeil * states that many of the Jansenist fanatics were subject to great illusions on this point; for many among them exhibited very obvious effects of the treatment, such as patches of discoloration on the skin, and innumerable contusions on the parts which had suffered the most severe assaults. Then it must be remembered that the blows upon the belly were given while the paroxysms were present, and when the stomach and intestines were distended with wind—a condition almost inseparable from the hysterical state. The prize-fighters of our own day, by filling the chest with air, endure blows which untrained persons could not receive without serious injury.

* *Op. cit.*, tome ii., p. 386.

The writer has had the opportunity of witnessing many manifestations of hysteria analogous in character to those described in the foregoing remarks. Upon one occasion a young woman, a patient in the wards of the Pennsylvania Hospital, began a series of movements consisting in bending her body backward till it formed an arch, her heels and head alone resting on the bed, and then, suddenly straightening herself out, would fall heavily. Instantly the arch was formed again; again she fell; and this process was kept up with inconceivable rapidity for several hours every day. In another instance, a lady, during an access of hysterical paroxysms to which she was liable, beat her head with such violence against a lath-and-plaster partition, that she made a hole in it, while little or no injury was inflicted on herself. In another, a girl eighteen years of age lay down on the floor, naked, and made all the members of her family, five in number, stand each in turn for several minutes on her abdomen. In another, a lady, in order that she might resemble those martyrs who suffered on the rack, tied her wrists with a stout cord, mounted a step-ladder, fastened the cord to a hook in the wall, and then, jumping from the ladder, succeeded in dislocating her shoulder. In another a lady rigidly closed her mouth, and refused to open it, either to take food or to speak, for over forty-eight hours. No force that it was safe to use could overcome the contraction of her muscles, and no persuasion induce her to relax them. She only yielded to an irresistible impulse to talk, and a degree of hunger that human nature could no longer endure. It would be easy to go on and cite, from the writer's practice or from monographs on the subject, hundreds of other instances of hysterical folly in which the subjects have been able to violate the laws of their being without apparently suffering serious pain or injury.

During the sixteenth and seventeenth centuries an epidemic of hysterical chorea with catalepsy prevailed in many convents of Europe, and many grievous wrongs were in consequence inflicted upon perfectly innocent persons whom the "possessed" accused of having bewitched them; among others, Louis Gaufridi, a priest of Marseilles, and a man of cultivation and strict morality, was accused by two Ursuline nuns, named Madeline de Mandol and Louise Capel, the latter but nineteen years of age. At the time of the accusation these women were suffering from attacks of an hysterical kind, accompanied with hallucinations and illusions, fearful convulsions and cataleptic paroxysms, all of which were ascribed to possession of the devil, moved and instigated by Louis Gaufridi. At first, the accused denied the charges made against him, and endeavored by arguments to show the true nature of the seizures. The effort was in vain; he became insane, and confessed all that was laid to his charge, with numerous other offences, which had not been imagined. He declared that he had worshipped the devil for fourteen years, and that " ce demon m'engagea à rendre amoureuses de ma personne toutes les femmes qui j'attendrois de mon souffle. Plus de milles femmes ont été empoisonnée par l'attrait irresistible de mon souffle qui les rendroit passionnées. La dame de la Pallude, mère de

Madeline, a été prise pour moi d'un insensée et s'est abandonnée à moi soit au sabbat soit hors du sabbat."

Gaufridi was burned at the stake, and the two Ursuline nuns "continuerent à délirer." * Among the convents visited by this terrible disorder was that of Sainte-Brigitte, at Lille. Several of the nuns had been present at the proceedings against Gaufridi, and had thus been subjected to influences readily capable of producing the disease.

Among the sisters was one named Marie de Sains, who was remarkable for her many virtues, but who was now suspected of devoting herself to sorcery and of being the cause of the "possessions" of which the other nuns were the victims. She remained a year in prison, without any formal proofs of her guilt being adduced, until at last she was positively accused by three of the sisters with having intercourse with demons. At first, the poor nun appeared to be surprised at this charge; but suddenly she recanted her denial, and avowed herself the perpetrator of a series of such wicked and abominable acts that it was difficult to understand how the conception of them had ever entered her mind. Among them were numberless murders, stranglings of innocent children, ravaging of graves, feeding on human flesh, revelling in orgies of superhuman atrocity, unheard-of sacrileges, poisonings, and in fact every imaginable crime. In the presence of her accusers and exorcists she improvised sermons which she ascribed to Satan, discoursed learnedly on the apocalypse, and made long

---

* Calmeil, De la Folie, etc. Paris, 1845, t. i., p. 489, *et seq.*

discourses on antichrist. Like others of the present day, she was a speaking medium.

Marie de Sains was not burnt. She was merely stripped of her religious character, and condemned to perpetual imprisonment at Tournay.

A more noted example of spiritual possession is that afforded by the nuns of Loudun, and which resulted in the death of Urban Grandier at the stake after he had been submitted to the most atrocious tortures, in the vain attempt to make him confess to an alliance with the devil.*

As showing the nature of the phenomena exhibited in the cases of monomania occurring among the nuns of Loudun, the following questions were proposed by Santerre, priest and promoter of the diocese of Nîmes, to the University of Montpellier:

Question 1. Whether the bending, bowing, and removing of the body, the head touching sometimes the soles of the feet, with other contortions and strange postures, are a good sign of possession ?

2. Whether the quickness of the motion of the head forward and backward, bringing it to the back and breast, be an infallible mark of possession ?

3. Whether a sudden swelling of the tongue, the throat and the face, and the sudden alteration of the color, are certain marks of possession ?

---

* For a very full account of this lamentable event, see the "Cheats and Illusions of Romish Priests and Exorcists discovered in the History of the Devils of Loudun. Being an Account of the Pretended Possession of the Ursuline Nuns, and of the Condemnation and Punishment of Urban Grandier, a Parson of the same Town." London, 1705.

4. Whether dulness and senselessness or the privation of sense, even to be pinched and pricked without complaining, without stirring, and even without changing color, are certain marks of possession?

5. Whether the immobility of all the body which happens to the pretended possessed by the command of their exorcists, during and in the middle of the strongest agitations, is a certain sign of a truly diabolical possession?

6. Whether the yelping or barking like that of a dog, in the breast rather than in the throat, is a mark of possession?

7. Whether a fixed, steady look upon some object, without moving the eye on either side, be a good mark of possession?

8. Whether the answers that the pretended possessed made in French, to some questions that are put to them in Latin, are a good mark of possession?

9. Whether to vomit such things as people have swallowed be a sign of possession?

10. Whether the prickings of a lancet upon divers parts of the body, without blood issuing thence, are a certain mark of possession?

All these questions, to the credit of medical science, were answered in the negative. No one can read them without being struck with the absolute identity of the symptoms, in all essential characteristics, with those which in our day are asserted to be due to spiritual possession, and with those met with in the various forms of hysteria. Cases almost exactly in point have already been cited in this essay.

Nor have these epidemics been restricted to convents or Catholic lands. Protestants of the straitest sects have been visited, and our own country has afforded many notable examples, besides possessing the doubtful honor of originating spiritualism in its present form.

The history of witchcraft, as it existed in New England during the latter part of the seventeenth century, is exceedingly instructive to the student of human nature, and of great interest in the present connection. As an illustration of the symptoms exhibited by the so-called " possessed "—the " mediums " of our day—I subjoin the following case, being the " ninth example " adduced by the Rev. Cotton Mather.* It would be difficult to select from all the records of medicine better examples of the blending of hysteria, chorea, and catalepsy. The evidence concerning the diabolical character of the " Quaker's book," " popish books," and the " Prayer-book," is incidentally, though with manifest gusto, thrown in by the narrator for what it is worth.

Four children of John Goodwin, of Boston, remarkable for their piety, honesty, and industry, were in the year 1688 made the subjects of witchcraft. The eldest, a girl about thirteen years old, had a dispute with the laundress about some linen that was missing, whose mother, a " scandalous Irishwoman of the neighborhood," applied some very abusive language to the child. The latter was at once taken with " odd fits,

* " Magnalia Christi Americana," etc. First American, from the London edition of 1702. Hartford, 1820, vol. ii., pp. 396.

which carried in them something diabolical." Soon
afterward the other children, a girl and two boys, became similarly affected. Sometimes they were deaf,
sometimes blind, sometimes dumb, and sometimes all
of these. Their tongues would be drawn down their
throats, and then pulled out upon their chins to a pro-
digious length. Their mouths were often forced open
to such an extent that their jaws were dislocated, and
were then suddenly closed with a snap like that of a
spring-lock. The like took place with their shoulders,
elbows, wrists, and other joints. They would then lie
in a benumbed condition, and be drawn together like
those tied neck and heels, and presently be stretched
out, and then drawn back enormously. They made
piteous outcries that they were cut with knives, and
struck with blows, and the plain prints of the wounds
were seen upon them.

[This latter is not an uncommon occurrence. I once
detected a woman cutting herself with a knife, and
thus inflicting wounds which she afterward declared
were given her by a spirit whom she had offended in
the flesh.]

At times their necks were rendered so limber that
the bones could not be felt, and again they were so
stiff that they could not be bent by any degree of force.

The woman who by her spells was supposed to have
caused these "possessions" was arrested. Her house
was searched, and several images made of rags and
stuffed with goat's-hair were found. These the woman
confessed she employed for the purpose of producing
the torments in the children, which she did by wetting

her finger with saliva and stroking the images. The experiment was made in court, to the entire satisfaction of all concerned. The woman, who was evidently insane, and probably rendered so by the accusations made against her, acknowledged that she was in league with the devil. She was tried, condemned to death, and executed. On the scaffold she declared that others remained who would carry on the work of tormenting the children; and so the calamities of the victims went on. They barked like dogs, purred like cats, at times complained that they were in a red-hot oven, and again that cold water was thrown on them. Then they were roasted on an invisible spit, and would shriek with agony; their heads they said were nailed to the floor, · and it was beyond ordinary strength to pull them up. They would be so limber sometimes that it was judged every bone they had might be bent, and then so stiff that not a joint could be flexed. And so the story goes on through several pages of details. Unseen ropes and chains were put around them, blows were given, and then the narrator continues, in regard to the eldest of the children, who was specially under his observation:

"A Quaker's book being brought to her, she could quietly read whole pages of it; only the name of God and Christ she still skipped over, being unable to pronounce it, except sometimes stammering a minute or two or more over it. And when we urged her to tell what the word was that she missed, she would say: 'I must not speak it. They say I must not. You know what it is. 'Tis G, and O, and D.' But a book against

Quakerism they would not allow her to meddle with. Such books as it might have been profitable and edifying for her to read, and especially her catechisms, if she did but offer to read a line in them, she would be cast into hideous convulsions, and be tossed about the house like a football. But books of jests being shown her, she could read them well enough, and have cunning descants upon them. Popish books they would not hinder her from reading, but they would from books against popery.

"Divers of these trials were made by many witnesses, but I, considering that there might be a snare in it, put a seasonable stop to this kind of business. Only I could not but be amazed at one thing. A certain prayer-book being brought to her, she not only could read it very well, but also did read a large part of it over, calling it her Bible, and putting a more than ordinary respect upon it. If she were going into her tortures, at the tender of this book, she would recover herself to read it."

Then she rode invisible horses, and continued other pranks till at last "one particular minister" (who seems to have been very negligent heretofore), "taking a peculiar compassion on the family, set himself to serve them in the methods prescribed by our Lord Jesus Christ. Accordingly, the Lord being besought thrice in three days of prayer, with fasting, on this occasion, the family then saw their deliverance perfected."

In the tenth example it is stated that one Winlock Curtis, a sailor, "was violently and suddenly seized in an unaccountable manner, and furiously thrown down

upon the deck, where he lay wallowing in a great
agony, and foamed at the mouth, and grew black in
the face, and was near strangled with a great lump
rising in his neck nigh his throat, like that which bewitched or possessed people used to be attended withal."
Winlock Curtis clearly had an epileptic fit, and the
lump spoken of was the well-known globus hystericus,
which few of my nervous readers have failed to experience at some time or other of their lives.

Finally, the epidemic spread with such rapidity, and
so many accused themselves of converse with the devil,
that the common-sense of the people put a stop to further executions. In the language of Mather, "Experience showed that the more there were apprehended,
the more were still afflicted by Satan, and the number
of confessions increasing did but increase the number of
the accused; and the executing of some made way for
the apprehending of others. For still the afflicted complained of being tormented by new objects, as the former were removed. So that those that were concerned
grew amazed at the number and quality of the persons
accused, and feared that Satan by his wiles had en-
wrapped innocent persons under the imputation of that
crime; and at last it was evidently seen that there must
be a stop put, or the generation of the children of
God would fall under that condemnation. Henceforth,
therefore, the juries generally acquitted such as were
tried, fearing they had gone too far before, and Sir William Phips, the governor, reprieved all that were condemned, even the confessors as well as others."

The epidemic, being thus let alone, died a natural

death, as would likewise be the case with the spiritualism of the present day, with similar treatment.

The vagaries of the Shakers and Jumpers of our own country, of the Whirling Dervishes and other sects of the Old World, and the contortions, trances, and beatifications of camp-meetings and revivals, are too familiar to require more than the passing remark that they all come under the present category.

In a recent work,* which may certainly be regarded as good spiritualistic authority, there is an account of a medium who was by turns under the influence of a good spirit, called "Katy," and of a bad one, whom she asserted to be a "sailor-boy." This latter took great delight in swearing through her, and in uttering such profane language as he had been accustomed to use on earth. Many manifestations of the power of both these spirits were given, until, to quote the words of the narrator:

"About 1846 a most singular and distressing phase of these phenomena was superadded to the rest, under what claimed to be the influence of the profane sailor. The girl's limbs in several directions would be thrown out of joint, and that with apparent ease, in a moment, and without pain. To replace them seemed to be either beyond the power or the will of her invisible tormentor, and Dr. Larkin [a weak-minded man whose servant she was], though an experienced surgeon, was often obliged

* Modern American Spiritualism: a Twenty Years' Record of the Communion between Earth and the World of Spirits (pp. 159). By Emma Hardinge. Second edition. New York. 1870.

to call in the aid of his professional brethren and two or three strong assistants.

"On one occasion the knees and wrists of the girl were thrown out of joint twice in a single day. These painful feats were always accompanied by loud laughter, hoarse and profane jokes, and expressions of exultant delight, purporting to come from the sailor, while the girl herself seemed wholly unconscious of the danger of her awkward situation. The preternatural feats of agility and strength exhibited on these occasions could scarcely be credited, and the frightfully unnatural contortions of the limbs, with which she became tied up into knots and coils, baffle all physiological explanation or attempts at description."

Can any person familiar with the vagaries of hysteria doubt for an instant that this girl was suffering from it, and that her condition was aggravated by the notoriety which she gained by her performances? In what respect do these so-called spiritualistic exhibitions differ from those which have been cited?

From the same volume* the following account is taken:

"Four silly, badly-educated girls, of ages ranging from fifteen to twenty, having gathered together at a friend's house to 'have a time with the spirits,' or in other words to trifle with spiritual manifestations, seated themselves around a table, and, after asking all manner of foolish questions, requested the spirits to take hold of them.

"The spirits at once complied; seized them, treated

* *Op. cit.,* p. 271.

3

them in the roughest manner, and, shaking them, caused
them to use the most violent actions and outrageous
language, etc. In this strait one of the dignitaries of
the mother church was sent for in haste to 'expel the
obsessing demons.' After the priest had arrived at the
scene of disorder, he put on his robes, got ready the
holy water, and approached the possessed girls in the
due formulæ proper to such occasions. After many
sallies with the holy fluid, and a vast number of incan-
tations, none of which produced the slightest effect, the
mediums at length charged upon him with such irresistible power and such capacity of finger-nails, that the
worthy *padre* fled precipitately, leaving the field in possession of the 'demons' and the spectators who had
gathered together to witness the 'exorcism.' The girls
still continued to be used roughly, by the discordant
spirits they had invoked, until the arrival of some of
their spiritualistic friends, by whose judicious passes and
gentle remonstrances with the spirits, they were instantly relieved."

That these " silly, badly-educated girls " were simply
hysterical, no one with even a superficial acquaintance
with the normal condition of the nervous system, and
the aberrations to which it may be subjected, can enter-
tain the slightest doubt. It is from just such persons
as these that the best mediums are obtained. That
such phenomena as they and the girl whose case was
previously quoted exhibited are regarded as spiritualistic, is sufficient of itself to throw discredit on all the
other alleged manifestations of the spirits. " *Falsum
in uno, falsum in omnibus.*"

At most of the spiritualistic meetings which the writer has attended there have been hysterical phenomena manifested by some of the men and women participating in the exercises. At a recent public exhibition of the kind he predicted, from their personal appearance, with perfect accuracy who of those assisting would be thus affected. The symptoms of disordered nervous action which the audience was invited to consider proofs of spiritual agency consisted of incoherent utterances and convulsive movements of the head, arms, and legs. In one case these symptoms became permanent for several months; a well-developed case of chorea or St. Vitus's dance was thus established. The patient finally came under the writer's care, and was only cured by the persistent administration of iron and strychnine —medicines which, with good food and fresh air, appear to possess more exorcising power than the formulæ of the good priest mentioned by Mrs. Hardinge.

In hysteria, hallucinations of the several senses are very common. Attention has already been directed to the fact that they may be produced by an excessive amount of blood circulating through the brain. Hysteria is always accompanied by an anæmic condition of the brain, and hence we have an illustration of the well-known fact that opposite pathological states may give rise to similar sets of symptoms. It frequently happens that, just before death from exhausting diseases, the brain, enfeebled with the other organs of the body, is deceived by hallucinations of sight and hearing.

The records of spiritualism abound with instances of spirits being seen by the faithful, and many of the cases are to be referred to the existence of hysteria.* From among numerous similar examples which have come under the professional care or observation of the writer, the following are adduced :

A young lady gave very decided evidence of suffering from mental aberration. She had imbibed the delusion that she had a " double," whom she saw almost constantly, and with whom she conversed whenever she pleased. At first she had been very much frightened, but gradually had become accustomed to her imaginary companion, and was lonesome and uncomfortable without her. There was no other well-marked delusion, though some of her absurd fancies partook more or less of that character. Headache was almost an inseparable symptom, as was likewise pain in the back, nausea, and constipation. Her menstrual function was deranged, and her whole aspect was that of a person whose physical powers were below par. Strychnia, iron, and whiskey, and a full, nutritious diet, were not long in banishing her delusional visitor, and in otherwise restoring her health.

A married lady consulted the writer for advice regarding hallucinations of sight and hearing, with which she had suffered for several months. It was only necessary for her to think of some particular person, living or dead, when she immediately saw the image of the person thought of, who spoke to her, laughed, wept, walked about the room, or did whatever other thing

* For a very philosophical account of hallucinations due to slight cerebral disturbance, the reader is referred to " An Essay toward a Theory of Apparitions," by John Ferriar, M. D.  London, 1813.

she imagined. In fact, to such an extent had her proclivity reached, that it was often impossible for her to avoid thinking of persons, and immediately having their figures brought to her perception.

At first she religiously believed in the reality of her visions, and that she really saw the spirits of the various individuals of whom she happened to think. But, as the hallucinations became more common, she lost her faith, and ascribed them to their true cause—disease. Upon examination, I found that she was preëminently of an hysterical type of organization, and was then laboring under other symptoms of its presence, besides the hallucinations. Thus she had hysterical paralysis of motion and sensation in the right leg, to such an extent that she could neither move it, nor feel a pin thrust through the skin; there was occasional loss of voice and of the power of speech, and tonic contractions of various muscles, especially of those of the fingers and toes. Her pulse was small and weak, her bowels obstinately constipated, her appetite capricious, and her complexion pale. Not the least of her afflictions was an almost perpetual headache. Under a suitable hygienic and medicinal treatment, this lady entirely recovered.

A young lady, whom I saw at Bridgeport, Connecticut, in consultation with my friends Drs. Hubbard and Ohnesorg, had hallucinations of sight, in conjunction with other symptoms of the hysterical condition.

Another, whom I visited in consultation with my friend Dr. Blakeman, of this city, constantly saw a man, armed with a gun, whom she called Peter, and with whom she carried on conversations. She described him in detail, and tried to make others see him.

## VI.

In catalepsy we have an affection which is well calculated to fulfil many of the requirements of spiritualism. It is characterized by suspension of the understanding and of sensibility, and by a tendency in the muscles to preserve any degree of contraction which may be given them. Thus, if the arm of a cataleptic patient be extended, it remains so for several minutes; if the leg be raised from the bed, the muscles continue to keep it in that position till they become thoroughly exhausted, when it sinks slowly down. Its causes are very similar to those which induce hysteria, with which it is closely allied and often blended. Among them emotional disturbance, a peculiar condition of the nervous system called by the French *nervosisme*, hereditary influence, excessive mental exertion, imitation, and a desire for notoriety, are the chief.

During the cataleptic condition, sensation is generally suspended. Pins can be thrust into the body and they are not felt, and even more severe injuries are not perceived; the eyes do not see, though the eyelids may be open; loud noises are not heard, penetrating odors are not smelt, or strongly sapid substances tasted. In uncomplicated catalepsy consciousness is lost; but in the mixed forms, which are much more common, the intellectual faculties are often exercised to a remarkable extent. Besides its hysterical affinities, catalepsy is correlative with ecstasy (a modified form), chorea, somnambulism, and epilepsy, and may pass, by insensible gradations, into either of these diseases.

In the less perfectly developed forms of the cataleptic condition, the affected individuals, though taking no cognizance of the circumstances surrounding them, are capable of a certain exalted esoteric mental action, which passes with the vulgar for illumination, inspiration, or spiritualization. Chambers * quotes from De Haen the case of a child twelve years old who began a paroxysm by being cataleptic and ended by reciting the metrical Protestant version of David's Psalms, saying her catechism with proof-texts, and preaching a sermon on adultery.

A young girl, recently under the professional care of the writer, was cataleptic, on an average, once a week, and epileptic twice or three times in the intervals. Five years previously she had spent six months in France, but had not acquired more than a very slight knowledge of the language, scarcely, in fact, sufficient to enable her to ask for what she wanted at her meals. Immediately before her cataleptic seizures she went into a state of ecstasy, during which she recited poetry in French and delivered harangues about virtue and godliness, in the same language. She pronounced at these times exceedingly well, and seemed never at a loss for a word. To all surrounding influences she was apparently dead. But she sat bolt upright in her chair, her eyes staring at vacancy, and her organs of speech in constant action. Gradually she passed into

* Reynolds's System of Medicine, p. 104 ; art. Catalepsy.

the cataleptic paroxysm. She was an excellent example of what Mrs. Hardinge calls a "trance medium."
The materialistic influence of bromide of potassium,
however, cured her of her catalepsy and epilepsy, de-
stroyed her knowledge of the French tongue, and made
her corporeal structure so gross that the spirits refused
to make further use of it for their manifestations.

Among celebrated cataleptics and ecstatics may be
mentioned Elizabeth of Hungary, St. Gertrude, St.
Bridget, St. Catharine of Sienna, Joan of Arc, St.
Theresa, Madame Guyon, and Joanna Southcote. The
conventual life was especially favorable to the production of all the forms of catalepsy, and sometimes, as in
the instance of the nuns of Loudun, the disease assumed a malignancy which all the power of the Church
could not abate.

It is a striking fact, which would be laughable, but
for the frequently lamentable results which ensued,
that while the Catholic ecstatics inveighed against the
heretical sects which were springing up on all sides,
and consigned them to torture and the flames, these,
the Calvinists, Camisards, Preadamites, Jumpers, Ana-
baptists, Quakers, Methodists, Tremblers, etc., etc., de-
nounced the Pope as anti-Christ, desecrated churches,
and exhibited a ferocity which in its sanguinary character has rarely been equalled.

Now, as has already been remarked, in the imper-
fect forms of catalepsy or ecstasy, consciousness is not
altogether lost. Montgeron noticed this fact, and, in
speaking of persons affected, says they generally see
those who are about them, speak to them, and hear

their answers, though, at the same time, their minds are apparently entirely absorbed in the contemplation of objects which a superior power enables them to see. It must be recollected that Montgeron was a believer in the supernatural origin of these manifestations of disease. At the present day he would have been a shining light among spiritualists.

He further observes, that in these undeveloped forms of the disorder, as noticed among the Jansenist Convulsionnaires, the affected individuals appeared as if struck by the sight of some object before unseen, and the contemplation of which filled them with the most ravishing joy. They raised their eyes and their hands on high, leaped toward heaven, and seemed as if about to fly into the air. They appeared to be absorbed in the contemplation of celestial beauties. Their faces were animated with a brilliant glow, and their eyes, which could not be closed during the continuance of the ecstasy, remained open and fixed on the spiritualized object upon which they gazed. They were in a manner transfigured; they appeared to be perfectly unlike their natural selves. Those who ordinarily were low and repulsive were changed so profoundly that they could not be recognized.

The following example is domestic, and is taken from the *Norfolk Beacon* of August 19, 1824. It was copied into other religious papers without the least doubt being expressed of its being produced by the " Spirit of God : " *

* " Observations on the Influence of Religion upon the Health and Physical Welfare of Mankind. By Amariah Brigham, M. D." Boston, 1835, pp. 305.

"A singular display of the goodness and power of Almighty God at a camp-meeting held at Tangier Island.

"Miss Narcissa Crippin, a highly-respectable young lady, nineteen years of age, and a zealous Christian, was, on the evening of the 15th instant, so operated upon by the Spirit of God that her face became too bright and shining for mortal eyes to gaze upon without producing the most awful feeling to the beholders. It resembled the reflection of the sun upon a bright cloud. The appearance of her face for the space of forty minutes was truly angelic, during which time she was silent, after which she spoke and expressed her happy and heavenly feelings, when her dazzling countenance gradually faded, and her face resumed its natural appearance. The writer of this paragraph was an eye-witness of the circumstance above stated—such a sight he never expected to behold with mortal eyes, and to give a true description of what would be beyond the ability of mortal man. While she remained in the situation above described she was seen by more than two hundred persons, a few of whom have subscribed their names hereto.

> "WM. LEE (Rev.),
> "WM. E. WISE,
> "JOHN BAYLY."

I have frequently seen this remarkable change induced in the faces of persons of both sexes. It appears to be directly due to a relaxation of all the muscles of the face concerned in expression, and is accompanied by suffusion of the eyes and dilatation of the pupils.

Undoubtedly the instances mentioned in the Bible as transfigurations (see Exodus xxxiv. 29–35; Matthew xvii. 1, 2; Mark ix. 2, 3; Luke ix. 29) were of this character.

About fifty years ago a very remarkable case of preaching-ecstasy, or, as it would now be called by some, "trance mediumship," occurred in this city in the person of a maiden lady of delicate health, named Rachel Baker. Dr. S. L. Mitchill took great interest in her case, and had her sermons reported by a stenographer and published. Miss Baker was the daughter of a respectable farmer in Onondaga County, New York, and had received a plain but substantial education. About the age of twenty her mind became much exercised on the subject of religion, and at length her health became seriously affected, and she fell into the habit of trance-preaching. Her parents were at first surprised at what they regarded as a most extraordinary gift, though they afterward became convinced that it was the result of disease, and accordingly brought her to the city of New York, in order that she might have the benefit of the best medical skill. Crowds flocked to hear her preach in this city, at the houses of different medical practitioners. Her discourses were highly respectable in point of style and arrangement, and were interspersed with Scripture quotations. After her health was restored, she lost her faculty of trance-preaching, and never regained it. She died in 1843.*

* Copland's Dictionary of Medicine (American edition), vol. i., art. Catalepsy, note by Dr. C. A. Lee.

## VII.

Occasionally persons have the power of voluntarily producing hallucinations of various kinds—a practice fraught with danger, for the time comes, sooner or later, in which they cannot get rid of their false perceptions. Goethe states that he had the power of giving form to the images passing before his mind, and upon one occasion saw his own figure approaching him. Abercrombie * refers to the case of a gentleman who had all his life been affected by the appearance of spectral figures. To such an extent did this peculiarity exist, that, if he met a friend in the street, he could not at first satisfy himself whether he saw the real or the spectral figure. By close attention he was able to perceive that the outline of the false was not quite so distinct as that of the real figure, but generally he used other means, such as touch or speech, or listening for the footsteps, to verify his visual impressions. He had also the power of calling up spectral figures at will, by directing his attention steadily to the conceptions of his own mind; and this either consisted of a figure or a scene he had witnessed, or a composition created by his imagination. But though he had the faculty of producing hallucinations, he had no power of banishing them, and, when he had once called up any particular person or scene, he could never say how long it might continue to haunt him. This gentleman was in the

* Inquiries concerning the Intellectual Powers, and the Investigation of Truth. Tenth edition. London, 1840, pp. 380.

prime of life, of sound mind, in good health, and engaged in business. His brother was similarly affected.

Several like cases have come under the professional observation of the author. In one, the power was directly the result of attendance at spiritual meetings, and of the efforts made to become a good "medium." The patient, a lady, was of a very impressionable temperament, and was consequently well-disposed to acquire the dangerous faculty in question. At first she thought very deeply of some particular person, whose image she endeavored to form in her mind. Then she assumed that the person was really present, and she addressed conversation to him, at the same time keeping the idealistic image in her thoughts. At this period she was not deceived, for she clearly recognized the fact that the image was not present.

One day, however, she was thinking very intently of her mother, and picturing to herself her appearance as she looked when dressed for church, on a particular occasion. She was reading a book at the time, and, happening to raise her eyes, she saw her mother standing before her, clothed exactly as she had imagined her. At first she was somewhat startled, and in her agitation closed her eyes with her hands. To her surprise she still saw the phantom, but yet, not being aware of the centric origin of the image, she conceived the idea that she had really seen her mother's spirit. In a few moments it disappeared, but she soon found that she had the ability to recall it at will, and that the power existed in regard to many other forms—even those of animals, and of inanimate objects.

During the spiritualistic meetings she attended, she could thus reproduce the image of any person on whom she strongly concentrated her thoughts, and was for a long time sincere in the belief that they were real appearances. At last she lost control of the operation, and was constantly subject to hallucinations of sight and hearing. She was unable to sleep, complained of vertigo, pain in the head, and of other symptoms indicating cerebral hyperæmia. The application of ice to her head, and other suitable medication, saved her from an attack of insanity. But her nervous system was for several months in a state of exhaustion, from which she rallied with difficulty.

A young lady has recently informed me that she is able to bring visually before her the images of the characters contained in any novel she may have been recently reading, or in any striking play she may have witnessed.

It is probable that many of the visions of Jerome Cardan, and Swedenborg, were voluntary productions. On this principle can be explained many of the instances of spiritualistic hallucinations which have been detailed by inquirers willing to be deceived.

## VIII.

One alleged phenomenon of spiritualism is of so remarkable a character as perhaps to require separate consideration, and that is, "levitation," or the faculty of rising in the air against the force of gravity. This has been claimed, not only for tables, chairs, and the like, but also for the human body. The records of witchcraft and spiritualism abound with instances of the kind. There is no doubt that they are due to hallucination, legerdemain, or actual fraud. A visit to a performance of any pantomime, such as that in which the Ravel family or Mr. George Fox takes a prominent part, will give an opportunity for seeing as striking manifestations in this direction as any of those attributed to the agency of spirits, and that in the full blaze of light. Without going into particulars in regard to the levitation of inanimate objects, I propose to consider at some length the alleged elevation of the human body by spiritual agency. The remarks made on this point will be found more or less applicable to the lesser alleged violations of natural law.

Before the present spiritual era, it was asserted by many persons, or claimed for them by credulous adherents, that they had been lifted from the ground without the aid of material agencies. It is contended by the spiritualists that there were cases similar in character to those now declared to be quite common. An inquiry into the history of these earlier instances will serve to enlighten us relative to those of our own time.

According to Philostratus, Apollonius * saw the Bramins of India rise in the air to the height of two cubits, and walk there without earthly support.

The authority is not very reliable, but the Bramins are well known to be preëminent in feats of legerdemain. A few years ago I saw a Colonel Stodare, who had resided in India, and who was exhibiting his

* Philostratus Vita Apollonii Tyaneus, lib. iii., cap. xx., 17.

skill in magic at Egyptian Hall, London, cause a female confederate to remain suspended in the air after a table on which she had been reclining was removed. Long wands were passed through the air above and below her without any support being detected other than a slender cane which she held in one hand, and which rested lightly on the floor. The trick is quite a common one among the Bramins, and was probably used to impress Apollonius, who was regarded as a god by his followers. The instance, however, is quoted by several spiritualistic writers as establishing the possibility of levitation.

In a recent work on spiritualism * by an anonymous writer, I find the following statement, which is taken without credit, however, from "Howitt's History of the Supernatural" (vol. i., p. 491, American ed.).

"Savonarola, before his tragical death at the stake, and while absorbed in devotion, was seen to remain suspended at a considerable height from the floor of his dungeon. The historical evidence of this fact, says Elihu Rich, in the 'Encyclopædia Metropolitana,' 'is admitted by his recent biographer.' "

Now, I do not know who is here referred to as the "recent biographer" of Savonarola, but the most recent as well as most thorough and reliable history of this great man is that of Villari,† and this is what

* Planchette, or the Despair of Science ; being a Full Account of Modern Spiritualism, etc.  Boston, 1869, p. 107.

† La Storia di Girolamo Savonarola e de' suoi Tempi, Narrata da Pasquale Villari con l' aiuto di Nuovi Documenti.  Firenze, 1859–'61.

A translation of this work, by Leonard Horner, was published in London, by Longmans, in 1863.

he says of Savonarola's last night in prison. If any such incident as levitation had occurred, Villari would certainly have referred to it:

"The night was already far advanced when he returned to his prison; sleep and weariness so overpowered him that, almost as a sign of love and gratitude, he laid his head on the knees of the good Nicolini, and soon fell into a short and light slumber, during which he appeared to smile and dream, so great was the serenity of his mind and soul."—(vol. ii., p. 204.)

The rest of the night was passed in prayer.

Now, there is not a word here about being carried up from the floor. Some biographer may have made the assertion quoted by the author of Planchette; but Villari, who is Professor of History in the University of Pisa, evidently discredits any such story. Savonarola may at times have entertained such a delusion, for he was of a highly-nervous temperament, and claimed that he was subject to visions which he imagined were real events. He had read and reread those parts of the Bible which treat of visions, angels, and apparitions; his mind had become strongly impressed with their truth, and his nervous temperament was agitated to an extreme degree. The dreams and visions of his childhood were multiplied, they constantly obtruded themselves before his mind, and at night he was scarcely ever free from them. Thus, as Villari remarks, "He passed whole nights on his knees in his cell, a prey to visions, by which he more and more exhausted his strength, continually excited his brain, and then ended in seeing in every thing a revelation from the Lord." [*]

* *Op. cit.*, vol. i, p. 295.

If, therefore, Savonarola had entertained the delusion that he was at times lifted from the floor, there would have been nothing surprising in the circumstance ; yet there is no credible evidence—Mr. Elihu Rich, Mr. Howitt, the author of " Planchette," and the " recent biographer," to the contrary notwithstanding—that he ever had this delusion.*

No one has done more to perpetuate the stories of saints rising in the air than Calmet,† and his statements are accepted at the present day by the too-willing followers of spiritualism without the least hesitation or inquiry, and generally at second or third hand.   Calmet was born in the year 1672, and lived, therefore, at a period when a belief in the supernatural was general. His education for the Church did not by any means tend to lessen the force of the credulity implanted in him by Nature.   Thus his work shows that he believed in magic and sorcery, witchcraft, familiars, spirits and elves, demons, vampires, the possibility of a man being in two places at the same time, that the bodies of excommunicated persons do not decay, etc.   He credited

---

* The statement comes originally from Mr. Rich, who makes it without giving the name of his authority.   It is contained in a section signed with his initials, in " *The Occult Sciences: Sketches of the Traditions and Superstitions of Past Times and the Marvels of the Present.*"   London, 1855, p. 202.   A work written by himself and Rev. Edward Lindley, W. Cooke Taylor, LL. D., and Mr. Henry Thompson.   I have consulted several biographies of Savonarola without finding any reference to the circumstances he relates.

† The Phantom World ; or, the Philosophy of Spirits, Apparitions, etc.   By Augustin Calmet.   Edited, with an Introduction and Notes, by Rev. Henry Christmas.   London, 1850.

in full the allegations made against Gaufridi, and approved of his punishment. The instances he adduces in support of all his beliefs are numerous, and perfectly convincing to those who are willing to accept any statements which appeal to their love of the marvellous without asking for the proof. What he says in regard to the rising of the human body in the air comes under the same category, and has no evidence in its favor stronger than that brought forward in support of his other views of supernatural phenomena.

The twenty-first chapter of his treatise is thus entitled : "Reasons which prove the Possibility of Sorcerers and Witches being translated to the Sabbath." After referring to instances in the Bible, he says :

"We have in history several instances of persons full of religion and piety who, in the fervor of their visions, have been taken up into the air, and remained there some time. We have known a good monk, who rises sometimes from the ground, and remains suspended without wishing it, without seeking to do so, especially on seeing some devotional image or hearing some devout prayer, such as *Gloria in excelsis Deo!* I know a nun to whom it has often happened to see herself thus raised up in the air to a certain distance from the earth. It was neither from choice nor from any wish to distinguish herself, since she was truly confused at it." It is not stated by Calmet that either of these instances was witnessed by him. He then innocently inquires :

"Was it by the ministrations of angels, or by the artifice of the seducing spirit who wished to inspire her with sentiments of vanity? or was it the natural effect of divine love, or fervor of devotion in these persons?

"I do not observe that the ancient fathers of the desert, who were so spiritual, so fervent, and so great in prayer, experienced similar ecstasies."

As Calmet remarks, the phenomena were only met with in the "new saints."

Of these "new saints," who have been lifted up by unseen powers, he gives the following list:

St. Philip Neri.

St. Catharine Columbina.

St. Ignatius Loyola.

St. Robert de Palentin.

St. Bernard Ptolomæi.

St. Philip Benitas.

St. Cajetanus.

St. Albert of Sicily.

St. Dominic.

St. Christina, who was raised up after death, was restored to life, and who was thereafter so light that she could run with great swiftness.

A nun, named Seraphina, in whom the tendency to rise was so great that six sisters could not hold her down.

St. Dunstan, Archbishop of Canterbury, who, it will be recollected, caught the devil by the nose with a pair of red-hot pincers, and at whose instigation, or at least connivance, Elgiva, the wife of Edwy, was so cruelly murdered.

St. Richard, abbot of St. Vanne de Verdun.

Father Dominic Carme Dechaux, who floated about in the air, and who, while in this position, was so light that he was blown about like a soap bubble.

It would be a needless piece of labor to search through the lives of the saints for the details of these asserted examples of levitation. They all rest upon the same kind of evidence, where there is any at all—the declarations of the subjects themselves, or of some of their followers. I have, therefore, selected a few of the more notable instances for more thorough investigation than Calmet thought it necessary to give.

St. Philip Neri, born in 1595. Of this saint Butler * says: "Gallonio testifies that the divine love so much dilated the breast of our saint in an extraordinary rapture, that the gristle which joined the fourth and fifth ribs on the left side was broken, which accident allowed the heart and the large vessels more play."

After this statement we are prepared for any thing —and need not, therefore, be surprised that " Gallonio mentions several extraordinary raptures with which the saint was favored in prayer, and testifies that his body was sometimes seen raised from the ground during his devotions some yards high, at which times his countenance appeared shining with a bright light."

To this account Butler † appends the following remarks in the form of a note:

" We find the same authentically attested of many

* Lives of the Primitive Fathers, Martyrs, and other Principal Saints. Compiled from Original Monuments and other Authentic Records. By the Rev. Alban Butler. Third edition. Edinburgh, 1799, vol. v., p. 345

† *Op. cit.* p. 348.

other servants of God.   St. Ignatius Loyola was sometimes seen raised in prayer two feet above the ground,
his body at the same time shining like light.   The like
elevations are related in the lives of St. Dominic, St.
Dunstan, St. Philip Benitas, St. Cajetan, St. Albert of
Sicily, B. Bernard Ptolomæi, institutor of the congre-
gation of Our Lady of Mount Olivet Aug. XXI., B.
Robert of Palentin Aug. XVIII. in the Bollandists,
of St. Francis of Assisium in his life by Chalippi, and
others.   Many of the authors of these lives, persons of
undoubted veracity, testify that they were eye-witnesses
of these facts.   Others were so careful and diligent writers that their authority cannot be questioned."

Butler cites several of the cases on the authority of
Calmet, whom he praises in the highest terms.   But, as
showing the difficulty with which he has accepted their
truth, yet not perceiving that he is using a two-edged
sword, he says:

"Ennapius, a Platonic philosopher, who, in 380,
wrote the lives of Porphyrius and Jamblichus, relates
that the latter was often raised ten cubits into the air,
and was seen surrounded with a bright light."   But
he denounces Ennapius as "credulous, malicious, and
unworthy of credit," as being inimical to Christianity,
and in fact as bad as Porphyrius and Jamblichus themselves.   I am, nevertheless, decidedly of the opinion
that the evidence in favor of the levitation of Jamblichus, the Neoplatonic philosopher, is fully as strong as
that adduced on the side of any Christian saint, monk,
nun, or medium.

Among the instances mentioned by Calmet is that

of St. Theresa. This very remarkable woman was born in 1515. From a very early age she was afflicted with frequent fits of fainting and violent pain at her heart, which sometimes deprived her of her senses; sharp pains were frequent through her whole frame; her sinews began to shrink up, and finally, in August, 1537, when she was in her twenty-third year, she fell into a lethargic coma or trance, which lasted four days. At one time she was thought to be dead, and her grave was actually dug. During this attack she bit her tongue in several places, and was for a long time unable to swallow; sometimes her whole body seemed as if her bones were disjointed in every part, and her head was in extreme disorder and pain.

As Madden * remarks, from whom these particulars are taken, though it is found in Butler,† and in he rautobiography: "It is impossible for a medical man to read this account of the occasional falling into a lethargic state, fits of fainting and swooning, violent spasms, pain at the heart, temporary loss of reason, shrinking of the sinews, oppression, with a profound sense of sadness, biting of the tongue in many places when out of her senses, inability to swallow any liquid, distortion of the whole frame as if all her bones were disjointed, subsequent inability to stir hand or foot for some time, and a generally-diffused soreness so as to be unable to bear being touched, without coming to the conclusion that the sufferer labored under physical disease of a low

---

* Phantasmata; or, Illusions and Fanaticisms of Protean Forms, productive of Great Evils. London, 1857, vol. i., p. 1818.

† *Op. cit.*, vol. x., p. 324, *et seq.*

nervous or gastric kind, with continuous fever probably complicated with epileptic tendencies."

There can be no doubt that she was of a highly-hys-
terical temperament, and was subject to paroxysms of
hysterical chorea, catalepsy, and epilepsy.   Her visions
became very frequent, and her raptures were even more
numerous.   In rapture, as she says, " the body loses
all the use of its voluntary functions, and every part
remains in the same posture, without feeling, hearing or
seeing, at least so as to perceive it."

During these raptures she was at times under the
impression that she was raised in the air.   Speaking of
the elevation of her soul, she says:

" Sometimes my whole body was carried with it so
as to be raised up from the ground, though this was
seldom.   When I had a mind to resist these raptures,
there seemed to me somewhat of a mighty force under
my feet, which raised me up that I knew not what to
compare it to." *

It is said, Bishop Ypres saw her thus lifted up.
The instance in question is similar in general features
to all the others recorded of enthusiastic saints and
other religious persons.   The organization of St. Theresa was such as to allow of her imagining any thing
as reality ; and the hallucination of being lifted up, as I
shall show hereafter, is one of the most common, experienced by ecstatics.

A case not referred to by Calmet is that of St.
Francis, of Assisium, whose life is contained in Butler's †

* Butler, *op. cit.*, vol. x., p. 359.        † Vol. x., p. 71.

collection. This self-denying and enthusiastic saint died in 1226. He constantly wore a hair-shirt, rarely ate any thing cooked, and, when he did, put ashes and water on it, slept on the ground with a piece of wood or stone for a pillow, never drank enough water to satisfy his thirst, when tormented by an occasional accession of sexual desire, stripped himself and rolled in the snow, and made large snow-balls which he clasped in his arms, imagined that during a state of exaltation he had been marked in the hands, feet, and side, in imitation of the wounds received by Christ during the crucifixion, and exhibited the scars—the stigmata of catalepsy, besides giving many other evidences of laboring under mental derangement. Among his miracles, was that of curing a man of a virulent ulcer of the face by kissing the sore. It is therefore not strange that levitation was among his powers. As Butler says: "The raptures and other extraordinary favors which he received from God in contemplation, he was careful to conceal from men. St. Bonaventure and other writers of his life assure us that he was frequently raised from the ground in prayer. F. Leo, his secretary and confessor, testified that he had seen him in prayer raised above the ground so high, that this disciple could only touch his feet, which he held and watered with his tears, and that sometimes he was raised much higher." * As F. Leo is shown by this extract to have been of an excitable and nervous temperament, we would scarcely be warranted in placing im-

* *Op. cit.*, p. 104.

4

plicit confidence in any statement he might make bordering on affirmation of a miraculous act.

The cases cited are attributed to the influence of the Holy Spirit or to angels. There is another class of examples which are supposed to be due to the agency of demons, witches, or other diabolical power. Thus, those who had made a compact with the devil always went to the Sabbath by supernatural agencies, and generally through the air astride of a broomstick.* Others are cited by Mather, in the work already referred to, and many are contained in other treatises on the "black art." The evidence in support of this category of instances is fully as strong as that in favor of the more orthodox variety. A very well-authenticated case— as authentication goes in such matters—is that "*concerning the witchcraft practised by Jane Brooks upon Richard Jones, son of Henry Jones, of Shepton Mallet.*"† Among other spells laid on this unfortunate youth, we are told that—

"On the 25th of February, between two and three in the afternoon, the boy living at the house of Richard Ifles, in Shepton Mallet, went out of the room into the

* Many of the older works on sorcery and witchcraft contain plates representing the departure to the Sabbath, and the orgies which took place there under the auspices of the devil. Among the most striking are the *Description de l'Assemblie des Sorciers qu'on appelle Sabbat* in *L'Histoire des Imaginations, extravagantes de Monsieur Oufle*, Paris, 1754, t. ii., and *Départ pour le Sabbat*, and other plates in the second edition of the *Dictionnaire Infernale*. Paris, 1826.

† Sadducismus Triumphatus, or a Full and Plain Evidence concerning Witches and Apparitions. By Joseph Glanvil. London, 1726, p. 285, *et seq.*

garden. Ifles his wife followed him and was within two yards, when she saw him rise up from the ground before her, and so mounted higher and higher till he passed in the air over the garden-wall, and was carried so aboveground more than thirty years [yards?], falling at last at one Jordan's door at Shepton, where he was found as dead for a time, but, coming to himself, told Jordan that Jane Brooks had taken him up by the arm out of Ifles his garden, and carried him in the air as is related." It is, perhaps, scarcely necessary to add that Jane Brooks was condemned and executed.

In all supposed instances of levitation such as have been cited, the true explanation may be made by referring them to one or other of the following causes:

1. *An hallucination on the part of the subject, or of those asserting themselves to have been witnesses.* As De Boismont * remarks : " The sensation of flying is rather common. Frequently, in dreams, we feel ourselves borne along with the rapidity of an arrow; we accomplish great distances, just lightly touching the ground. We have noticed this fact in a literary man of our acquaintance, whom we have several times found, with fixed eyes, and who said to us, 'I am flying; do not stop me.' On returning to himself he described his sensations, and it seemed to him that he really had flown. This sensation was experienced as far back as the time of St. Jerome, who relates that, frequently, in his dreams, he felt himself flying over mountains, seas, etc.

---

* A History of Dreams, Visions, Apparitions, Ecstasy, Magnetism, and Somnambulism. American edition, Philadelphia, 1855, p. 94.

"Madame d'Arnim, Goethe's friend, in speaking of this fact, says: 'I was certain that I flew and floated in the air. By a simple, elastic pressure of the toe I was in the air. I floated silently and deliciously at two or three feet above the earth: I alighted, mounted again, I flew from side to side, and then returned. A few days after, I was taken with fever. I went to bed and slept. It happened two weeks after I was confined.'" *

Numerous other instances of similar cases are recorded in works on psychological medicine, and several have come under my own observation.

In one of these, a lady, of strongly-marked hysterical temperament, and of almost fanatical religious tendencies, imagined that she was frequently raised from the ground while in the act of saying her prayers. She usually spent several hours each day in these exercises, and during the whole time was in a state of fervid exaltation, which rendered her insensible to all that was passing around her. While in this condition she would exclaim, "I rise, I rise! I see angels!" and, with her hands raised on high, her head elevated, her face turned upward, and her countenance illuminated with ecstatic radiance, she really did seem, to some superficial and sympathetic observers, to be lifted up. Among others, her maid was strongly convinced that the elevation was actual; but stronger-minded members of her family could see nothing of the kind, and eventually the lady herself became convinced that she was the victim of self-deception. A young married lady, now under my

* Correspondence de Goethe et de Bettina. Translated by M. Sebact Albin, t. i., p. 68.

professional care, is very confident that, during the cataleptic seizures to which she is subject, she is raised from her bed, and she appeals with confidence to those surrounding her to confirm her statements. It almost always happens that some one present expresses the opinion that she really was lifted up several inches.

The majority of the cases met with in the lives of saints belong to this category. Nearly all the subjects were the victims of some severe disorder of the nervous system, by which they were rendered peculiarly susceptible to hallucinations; and their more ardent followers were either similarly affected or were so impressed by the power of suggestion, already considered in this essay, as to be fit recipients of erroneous mental or sensorial impressions.

The appearance as if about to fly is very common in cases of ecstasy, and is due to the raising of the arms, the upward look, and the elevation of the body on the extreme points of the toes. This position is sometimes kept for hours, and may readily—as the stature is increased in height—lead to the opinion that the body is off the ground, especially in the cases of women whose feet cannot readily be seen, owing to the drapery of their dress.

A sensation as if the body were passing rapidly through the air is induced by certain drugs, particularly aconite.

2. *Unintentional exaggeration, misinterpretation, and inaccuracy of statement.* It frequently happens that, during hysterical convulsions, the affected person makes strong efforts to rise, which attempts are strenu-

ously resisted by the bystanders. In former times, when every seizure of the kind was regarded as being directly due to the agency of demons, or other supernatural beings, acting either within the sufferer (possessive) or from without (obsessive), the idea was very naturally entertained that, but for the assistance of friends at hand, severe injury would result from the convulsive movements. When, therefore, the limbs were thrown about, or the body writhed, or the tongue was bitten, the afflicted epileptic, cataleptic, or hysterical individual was at once seized, and the statement made that all the phenomena of the paroxysm were caused by some kind of spiritual power. At the same time the actual violence of the manifestations was always over-estimated, just as is invariably done by spectators of our own day. It thus often happened that a contortion of the body was regarded as the effort of a demon to carry it off. No sensible person can read the accounts of witchcraft which have come down to us, and some of which have been cited in this essay, without being convinced that this was a frequent interpretation of well-known pathological symptoms, or doubt that several of the asserted instances of levitation—as, for instance, that of Sister Seraphina—are to be explained in a similar manner.

3. *Insufficient evidence.* Most of the instances of levitation which are recorded rest on insufficient evidence, such as would be inadequate to establish the fact in a court of law. This is the case, for example, with several of the alleged instances occurring in the persons of saints, monks, and nuns. It does not appear that

Calmet ever saw the human body lifted up without material agency, although he refers to several cases of which he had heard. Hearsay testimony is of so equivocal a character as to be disregarded in all matters of importance, and yet we are expected to rely on it as sufficient to establish the fact of miraculous events, which, of all others, should require the most unerring and irrefragable demonstration.

Take, for example, the alleged elevation of Savonarola, which is quoted with peculiar unction by the spiritualists of the present day. Research shows that the story is altogether of comparatively recent origin, and that its truth has been assumed by interested believers in supernaturalism, without due pains being taken to verify its accuracy.

And so, relative to St. Ignatius Loyola, whose elevation in the air is also a *point d'appui* for the spiritualists. A recent biographer, a sincere and devout member of the Roman Catholic Church, thus speaks of St. Ignatius and his faithful adherents, in connection with a report—the last of the kind—that a supernatural light had been seen around his body :

"His children never claimed for him a power of working prodigies, and he would certainly greatly have regretted such an attitude. All the remarkable circumstances of the kind that it has been thought right to detail may be set aside, if the reader so pleases. The true and only miracle that it is necessary to know and to appreciate is that of a most noble, extraordinary, and original character and an admirable life." *

* Ignatius Loyola and the Early Jesuits. By Stewart Rose. London, 1870, p. 481.

We know that even undoubted events, when seen through the prejudiced historian's spectacles, become so changed in character as to be scarcely recognizable, and that no two persons witnessing a transaction will give precisely the same version of it. Even in so exact a science as chemistry authorities differ, and, in testing for poisons, one observer has perceived the looked-for reaction, while another, working under the same conditions, has failed to see the change of color or the precipitation. The sensorial impressions of some persons are always modified by their mental bias.

4. *Intentional misstatement.* Some of the instances are probably due to misrepresentation, with the view of enhancing the reputation for sanctity of the subjects, or simply from that love for telling marvellous stories which is so inherent a quality with the majority of mankind ; such, in all likelihood, are the earlier examples— as that of St. Dunstan.

The cases, too, recorded in connection with witchcraft are many of them clearly fraudulent in character, fabricated for the purpose of injuring some obnoxious person by the imputation of being a witch. The boy who asserted, in conjunction with the wife of Ifles, that he had been carried over a wall by one Jane Brooks, was evidently in a conspiracy with Mrs. Ifles to accomplish the destruction of an innocent woman.

5. *Legerdemain.* This explanation has already been commented upon in connection with the Braminical exploits made before Apollonius Tyaneus ; that it is sufficient to account for many instances cannot be questioned.

The modern instances, attributed directly to the influence of the spiritualists, are scarcely deserving of mention. None of them are well authenticated, and all are more reasonably explained by ascribing them to one or several of the causes specified. Performed in the dark, they afford abundant opportunity for deceit on the one part, and hallucination or illusion on the other. They do not even claim to be as powerful manifestations as those specially referred to in this essay, for the latter were asserted to be done in broad daylight, and the subjects could be touched by those present; while those of our day avoid inquiry, and are performed under such circumstances as to defy thorough examination. In one case which came under my notice, the medium, a woman, was bound in a chair and seated at one end of a long table. The lights were then extinguished, and a blanket hung over the window, so as to exclude the feeblest ray of light from a dark night. The company, *with the exception of the medium's husband*, sat around the table, holding each other's hands. The only inquirers present were myself and another gentleman, who were carefully sandwiched between the faithful, who kept up a dismal howling while the experiment went on. The husband stood at one end of the room, outside of the circle. There was a good deal of noise at the medium's end of the table, which was only partially drowned by the lugubrious singing. Suddenly she exclaimed, "Now!" The gas was turned on, and she was found seated in the middle of the table still fastened to the chair; all present except my friend and myself were convinced that the spirits had placed her there.   We were not, for the reasons, mainly, that it was entirely practicable for her husband to have put her on the table without his movements being known to us, and that it was very easy, as I have ascertained by experiment, for her to have climbed to the top of the table without any assistance whatever.

There are perhaps fifty cases of levitation on record. I will engage to supply more and better-authenticated instances of any other hitherto-mentioned supernatural phenomenon—such as lizards living in the human stomach, persons walking without their heads, people with glass-legs, others who are coffee-pots; or, to go to the very opposite, instances of the force of gravity or the power of spirits being so great as to prevent the body being raised at all.   At the time of writing this, a lady is under my care who declares that she cannot rise from her chair, and who has succeeded in convincing several of her friends that she speaks the truth.   It would be easy to discover, by searching in the right places, many other cases of the kind, and here is one in point which I get at second-hand, as the spiritualists do theirs :

"In the northern borders of England, and on the other side of the river Humber, in the parish of Hovëden, lived the rector of that church with his concubine. This concubine one day sat rather imprudently on the tomb of St. Osanna, sister to King Ofred, which was made of wood, and raised above the ground in the shape of a seat.   When she attempted to rise from the place her posteriors stuck to the wood in such a manner that she never could be parted from it till, in the presence of the people who ran to see her, she had suffered her clothes to be torn from her, and had received a severe discipline on her naked body, and that to a great effusion of blood, and with many tears and devout supplications on her part. Which done, and after she had engaged to submit to further penitence, she was divinely released." *

A remedy so potent in gravitation would probably prove equally efficacious in levitation.


## IX.


At all times during the historic period, two classes of individuals have been concerned in the propagation of false ideas relative to the phenomena which it is now attempted to impose upon the world as produced by the agency of spirits. These are the deceivers and the deceived. Whether as priests, witches, magicians, mesmerizers, somnambulists, ecstatics, hysterical persons, or mediums, the first are deceivers; some of them honest, but, by far the greater number guilty of intentional fraud. Whether subject to illusions, hallucinations, or delusions, weak-minded or ignorant, the second are deceived.

In the foregoing pages the writer has attempted to

* The History of the Flagellants, otherwise of Religious Flagellations among Different Nations, and especially among Christians. Being a Paraphrase and Commentary on the Historia Flagellantium of the Abbé Boileau, Doctor of the Sorbonne, etc. By one who is not a Doctor of the Sorbonne [De Lolme]. The second edition. London, 1783, p. 317. The miracle referred to is quoted from the " Itinerarium Cambriæ, wrote by Sylvester Geraldus, a native of the country of Wales, who wrote about the year 1188."

give an outline view of some of the causes which produce many so-called supernatural manifestations, and which lead to their acceptance by certain classes of individu-als. To describe, in detail, all the vagaries of spiritualism would be a fruitless undertaking. He has witnessed many spiritualistic performances, and has never seen a single one which could not be accounted for by the operation of some one or more of the causes specified. No medium has ever yet been lifted into the air by spirits, no one has ever read unknown writing through a closed envelope, no one has ever lifted tables or chairs but by material agencies, no one has ever been tied or untied by spirits, no one has ever heard the knock of a spirit, and no one has ever spoken through the power of a spirit other than his own.

Even if bodies had been raised in the air by agencies unexplainable, even if some one had read writing through several thicknesses of paper, even if others had been bound and unbound in a way unknown to us, even if knocks had been heard whose sources could not be ascertained, even if the causes of all the phenomena of spiritualism were entirely beyond our present knowledge, there would be no proof that spirits had any thing to do with them. On the contrary, the hypothesis of spirits is altogether the least plausible which could be suggested. The phenomena and the explanation have nothing in common.

Spiritualism is a religion. As such it is held tenaciously and honestly by many well-meaning people. To reason with these would be a waste of words, just as much as would be the attempt to persuade a madman out of his delusion. Emotion or interest or accident might change them, but facts never. But there are some who halt between belief and unbelief, for the reason mainly that they have no clear conception of what knowledge is, and of how things are to be proved. For these there can be no more striking truths than the following account of Algazzali's description of his search for actual knowledge:

" The true source of casual beliefs is the authority of parents and preceptors. Now, there are many methods of comprehending the differences which exist between things received on the faith of such authority and the principles of the things themselves. There exist likewise many means of distinguishing the true from the false. For this reason I said to myself in the very beginning of my inquiry, ' My object is simply to know the truth of things, consequently it is indispensable to seek for that which constitutes knowledge.' Now, it is evident to me that certain knowledge ought to be that which explains the object to be known, so that there can be no doubt, and that all error and all conjecture would be henceforth impossible. And not only then the understanding would not need to make efforts to arrive at certainty, but the security against error ought to be in so intimate a connection with the thing known for certain, that even when an apparent proof of its falsity is produced—as, for example, if a man should transform a stone into gold or a stick into a serpent—no error should be caused, or even the suspicion of error rendered possible. If, when I have satisfied myself that ten is more than three, some one should say to me,

5

' Not so, on the contrary three is more than ten, and to prove to you the truth of my assertion I will transform this rod into a snake ; ' if then he should so transform it to my entire conviction, the certainty I should have of his error would not be shaken. His performance would produce in me only an admiration for his skill, but I should not doubt the truth I had acquired.

" Then I was convinced that all knowledge which I did not possess in this manner, and of which I had not this kind of certitude, could inspire me with neither confidence nor assurance, and that all knowledge without assurance is not a sure knowledge." *

How little the phenomena of spiritualism are reconcilable with the tests laid down by Algazzali every candid, intelligent, and educated inquirer knows.

* Essai sur les Écoles philosophiques chez les Arabes et notamment sur la Doctrine d'Algazzali.  Par Auguste Schmölders, Docteur en Philosophie.  Paris, 1842.

THE END.